HIGH 1 ᴧᴇST FARM

SALLY MARSH

High Forest Farm

This book is a work of fiction. Any references to historical events, real people, or real places are used fictitiously. Other names, characters, places, and events are products of the author's imagination, and any resemblances to actual events or places or persons, living or dead, is entirely coincidental.

Formatted by Frostbite Publishing

This book is dedicated to all the stolen and missing dogs that are still to find their way home and to their amazing owners who have never given up hope.

Below is a poster of Fern who belongs to Jodie Ferrier. Fern was stolen on 28th April 2013 from her home in Chessington. Please support her Facebook page 'Find Fern'.

GENDER: Female   BREED: Cocker X Springer Spaniel   AGE: Adult

MISSING SINCE: 28th April 2013   MISSING FROM: Rushett Farm, Chessington, KT9

MICROCHIPPED: Yes

MORE INFO: White chest, docked tail, wearing red collar with blue ID tag

© Pandoras In Need

The little dog trotted out of the open wooden back door and on to the dew-kissed grass of the lawn. Her stumpy tail wagged with delighted interest as she made her way to the tall back gate, sniffing excitedly along the way.

A rustling noise beyond the gate immediately caught her attention. Tipping her head to one side in curiosity the little dog waited and listened for the sound again.

Over the top of the gate a man's rough hand felt it's way along until it found the cold, metal bolt. As the man gently eased the gate open the little dog backed up nervously.

The gate opened to reveal a person she didn't recognise so the little dog let out a low growl followed by a sharp bark as a nervous warning to him. The man quickly threw a piece of fresh meat at her feet and, with only slight hesitation, she ate it hungrily.

The man offered her a second piece of meat in his outstretched hand.. The little dog happily approached and gently took it from him, in a flash he grabbed her collar and scooped her up into his strong arms. She yelped in fright, but before she could struggle too much, the man climbed into the front seat of a waiting van and sped off down the road with her, leaving the gate wide open.

From the house a lady, wrapped in a dressing gown and slippers, peered out of the door into the now empty garden. Spotting the open gate, she whistled and called the little dog's name, waiting for her familiar face to appear, but it didn't. Calling again and again she ran to the gate and looked down the road but it was too late, the road was empty and the little dog had vanished..

CHAPTER 1

The fox stopped mid-stride and sniffed the frosted ground, his rust-red fur and white-tipped tail standing out against the frozen grass.

As his ears flicked around listening out for possible dangers, his senses picked up movement across the field. With a black-tipped paw lifted slightly off the ground, he was ready to run. Lowering his body he tiptoed towards the safety of the bramble hedge and paused again. In the far corner of the field a small black shape slowly picked its way across the cold grass like a shadow as it headed for the warm glow of the Farm House

This morning the small back shape had got closer than it ever had before until a door shutting spooked it once again, sending it bolting back to the dark safety of the woods.

Wearing a brightly coloured wooly hat with an oversized pompom on the top and a fleece jacket zipped up over half her face Jenna Waters jogged across the small lawn and down towards the field gate, pulling on a pair of oddly matched gloves as she went.

This was part of her morning routine now as she went down to feed her beloved horse Snow Prince, before heading for the school bus.

The grey gelding banged his stable door as he saw her approach, his hot breath mixing with the freezing air made him look half horse and half dragon.

"OK, OK I'm coming" Jenna tutted, as she struggled with the bolt on the tack room door. Yanking the warped door open, she grabbed a spare bucket from the neatly stacked pile in the corner and proceeded to fill the bucket with sweet smelling chaff from a metal dustbin. Humming as she went about her task, Jenna opened up the second dustbin and let out a shriek as a small brown field mouse leapt out.

"Every time!" she laughed as the terrified mouse shot out through a hole in the wooden walls. Her brother Ed wanted to set a mouse trap but Jenna had been adamant that there was no way he would be harming any animals on the farm, pest or otherwise!

Scooping a heap of pony nuts into the bucket and giving it a quick mix with a wooden spoon she shuffled back out of the door to feed the impatient horse. Reaching his door she patted his outstretched neck and laughed as he tried to grab the bucket with his teeth.

"Just wait will you?" She hissed, as she unbolted his door and with a firm voice told him to "Back up" as she went in. Tipping his feed into the manger she smoothed his soft neck and adjusted his rug slightly as he ate.

The last few months had been a whirlwind of new experiences for the pair of them. When Snow Prince had arrived from the auction the pair had formed a strong bond and a mutual respect for each other. From the moment Jenna had laid eyes on the gelding that day as he lay helpless on the road, she had known he was special and now as he stood in the stable she still couldn't believe he was hers!

Snow Prince had been so nervous when he had arrived and Jenna had spent hours sitting in the field reading books just to get him used to her being around. She was sure her parents thought she was mad but she didn't care! Her tactics had worked and after a few days Snow Prince would sneak up behind her and nudge her back gently, so she would carefully hold out a treat to him on a quivering hand. Soon he had started following her around the field and would let her scratch his chest which resulted in him sticking his top lip out in appreciation.

In no time she and her friend Victoria, who owned the Red Fox Pub, had been able to easily clip a rope onto his headcollar and walk him a short way round the field. Now he would stand happily in the stable and be groomed from head to toe, although the first time the farrier had visited he hadn't quite been on his best behaviour! Jenna had worried the poor chap wouldn't come again but she had worked hard on the gelding's tickly legs and he had behaved like a pro when the farrier returned, much to her relief!

Leaning on the stable door watching him eat Jenna felt so lucky. She had always dreamed of owning her very own horse and now she did. As she day dreamed a rustling noise behind her made her jump slightly. Spinning round to see what had made the noise she was puzzled to find there was nothing there.

"Must be the wind" she muttered, checking her

watch, she decided that she was running short of time, so, grabbing Snow Prince's headcollar and lead rope, she quickly slipped it on his elegant head and led him out of his stable and to the paddock

As soon as she unclipped the lead rope the gelding shot off bucking and wheeling in the same way he did every morning.

"You are such a Clown" Jenna tutted and shutting the gate firmly behind her, she jogged back to shut the stable door, then ran back to the warmth of the house. As she reached the door she turned back for a last look at Snow Prince and spotted something moving along the far hedgerow.

Squinting to try and get a better look, she lost sight of whatever it was. She was sure there had been something there but running late as usual she just shrugged her frozen shoulders and shut the door. From the safety of the thick hedge a pair of shining black eyes watched Jenna disappear inside before creeping back towards the darkness of the woods.

CHAPTER 2

J enna was convinced she had seen something in the paddock that morning and after what seemed like the longest day at school, she decided that as soon as she got home she would go and investigate further.

Snow Prince was still busy munching grass as she walked down towards the paddock but he suddenly stopped and looked up towards the woods appearing to be intently watching something. Jenna started to walk towards him and soon his attention turned to her.

"What have you spotted then boy?" She whispered as she ran her fingers through his tangled forelock and down his soft face, his warm breath flushing across her fingers as she reached his nostrils.

Peering towards the woods it was hard to see what he had been staring at but Jenna was sure that something was making a home in the woods. Feeling even more curious she headed over to the edge of the trees, occasionally pausing as she went to see if she could pick up any sounds. Perhaps it was the Roe deer which could often be seen eating alongside Snow Prince, although what Jenna had seen in the morning had been most definitely black in colour.

Climbing through the fence she kept her eyes fixed on the ground, looking for signs of tracks in the muddy ground but with a carpet of flame coloured fallen leaves it was impossible to see anything. In the center of the woods stood a huge old oak tree which years ago had been struck by lightning and almost split in two. At its base the split arched up in a twisted fashion leaving a large hole which went deep into the tree. As she peered in Jenna spotted that there were quite a few pieces of rubbish tucked away into it. The rubbish included old meat packets and bread wrappers which had been torn apart to get to whatever remaining food was inside. Was a fox using the tree to live in she wondered? Jenna was still not convinced as foxes usually lived in a den deep underground.

Collecting all the rubbish up she continued to search the woods. Suddenly to her left something took off at speed through the thick brambles making Jenna jump out of her skin. Getting herself together Jenna ran in the direction of the noise and as she reached the boundary fence she caught sight of the animal making the noise as it crossed the neighbour's adjoining field.

It was a dog!

Running flat out across the stubble the dog never looked back until it had reached the fence on the other side. Jenna tried whistling but that just seemed to spook the dog more and it disappeared out of sight again. What was a dog doing living in the woods? And who did it belong to? Jenna was both puzzled and concerned as to why it was so frightened. As she walked back through the woods she paused at the tree again. Was the dog really living in there? She had to find out.

Reaching the stables she grabbed tools and a wheelbarrow and started to muck out Snow Prince's stable. As she picked out the droppings and tidied the bed ready for the horse she kept pausing and looking out, back towards the woods for the dog but sadly there was no sign of it. Finishing the straw bed and refreshing his water Jenna went back out into the paddock to bring Snow Prince in. Tying him up outside the stable, she collected some brushes from the tack room and proceeded to try and make the gelding look respectable again.

As she bent down to brush his muddy legs Jenna caught sight of something moving in the hedge again. It was the dog! Jenna paused, trying not to move as her legs started to ache from holding the same position.

The dog crept from the hedge and it stood stock still, staring straight at Jenna. Slightly concerned that the dog might not be horse-friendly, Jenna quickly stood up and put Snow Prince into the safety of the stable. As she looked for the dog in the field again she found it had once more disappeared. With her heart beating just a little faster Jenna slowly walked out across the paddock again, but with the winter sun fading fast everything looked like a black dog shaped possibility as the darkness crept in.

CHAPTER 3

As she sat at the large wooden kitchen table eating dinner with her family, Jenna's mind wandered back to the thought of the dog living in the woods. Should she tell her parents what she had seen? She wasn't sure if she should as knowing her parents they would want to call the local dog warden or local rescues which might frighten the dog more. She wanted to find out more about the dog herself first and try and gain its trust a little. It had clearly been living in the woods for a few days as it had raided the rubbish bags her Dad had left out 4 days ago.

Jenna needed to think of a plan to get closer to the dog and she figured food might be the answer. Offering to clear the dinner plates from the table, much to her parent's surprise, she carefully carried them to the kitchen where, as quietly as she could, she scraped the leftover food into an old lunch box. Grabbing her jacket and a torch, she called to her parents to say she was just off to check on Snow Prince. Crunching across the already frozen grass Jenna kept the torch pointed low onto the ground, if the dog was nearby she didn't want to frighten it.

An owl screeching somewhere close by made her jump and she dropped the torch and was suddenly plunged into darkness as its batteries spilled out onto the frozen ground.

"Jeezzz" through her chattering teeth, Jenna fumbled for the batteries as they glinted in the frosty moonlight. Finally getting them back into the torch in the right order Jenna jogged quietly towards the stables, although her approach wasn't totally silent because as soon as Snow Prince heard her coming he let out a loud welcoming neigh!

"Sssshhh" she hissed at him "If that poor dog is around it won't be for long with all your racket!" He did make her laugh, gone was the semi-wild pony who had arrived a few months ago and in its place was a carrot munching pampered pet!

Turning her attention to the barn doors, Jenna eased open one of the heavy wooden doors and propped it open with a length of wood. Shining her torch around she found what she was looking for, an old metal tray. Wiping off the worst of the dust she laid it in the entrance of the barn and tipped the scraps of food on to it. Her plan was to encourage the dog to come to the barn with food as she knew it was obviously very hungry. Whether her plan would work she didn't know but it was worth a go.

As she turned to leave she heard a sound that made her stop in her tracks. Slowly turning round she slowly raised the torch beam towards the noise which sounded like a gentle thumping. A pair of eyes lit up in the torch light! It was the dog!

Jenna was unsure what to do next but as the thumping sound started again she realised it wasn't the sound of her heart beating rapidly in her chest, it was the dog's tail wagging rapidly.

"Hello Sweetie" she whispered, her voice cracking slightly with nerves. Taking a step closer to the dog Jenna felt a little braver as the dog continued to wag its stumpy tail.

As she took another step the dog started to turn and head back away from her so she stopped and backed up herself. Turning slowly around she walked a little distance and stopped to look again. The dog's eyes gleamed in the torch beam again so Jenna turned the beam to shine on the tray of food.

"Come on" she whispered, "I bet you're hungry?" she carried on whispering, her teeth chattering from the cold night air. The dog just stood looking at her but after a few seconds it crept forward, its nose twitching and sniffing along the concrete towards the tray. Jenna held her breath as the dog took a huge bite of food and bolted off back into the darkness.

Letting out a long held in breath Jenna realised her hands were shaking and it wasn't just from the cold! She hadn't quite counted on the dog appearing so quickly, it must be starving? Had it watched her whilst she fussed Snow Prince? Deciding she had better head back to the house before her parents sent out a search party, Jenna trudged back to the warmth of the kitchen with her mind still firmly on what to do about the dog. Would it come back and finish the leftover food and then sleep in the barn? Jenna hoped so. She now planned to do the same thing every evening in the hope of gaining the dogs trust.

Opening the door to the kitchen she was met by a rush of warm air and quickly went and held her hands over the Aga while she attempted to get feeling back in her fingers. As she did her Mum came in carrying a basket of washing.

"All OK love?" She smiled. "Was Snow Prince settled enough?"

Jenna, trying to look a little less frozen, nodded.

"He was fine thanks, I just wanted to check he was warm enough." Then changing the subject to the fact she had homework to do, she made her excuses and headed up to her bedroom.

Lying on her bed Jenna started to think about the little dog. It looked like a spaniel type although she had only got short looks at it. She was still puzzled as to how it had turned up on the farm. She decided that tomorrow at school she would tell her best friend Zoe about it. Perhaps she would know of someone who had lost a dog in the area?

Grabbing her laptop Jenna quickly turned it on and logged onto the internet and after doing a search for their area Jenna could find nothing about a lost dog matching the dog in the woods anywhere near to Brannton. With a new law being brought in that every dog must be microchipped, she knew that to find out where the dog was from she would first have to catch it and get it scanned by the local Vet in the hope that it was microchipped and that its owner could be traced. The only problem was how would she catch it?

CHAPTER 4

Waking up extra early the next morning, Jenna quickly dressed and crept out of the silent house while the rest of the family were still asleep. Pulling on thick fleece gloves and her bobble hat she quickened her step towards the stable keeping a close eye out for the dog as she went.

Snow Prince shouted his normal greeting as he saw her approach so any hope of her creeping down to the barn unnoticed were shattered. Approaching the tray Jenna immediately spotted it was empty and she hoped that the dog had been back and finished the rest of the food and not the local fox!

Snow Prince started to impatiently bang his door with his hoof and Jenna hissed at him to stop it, not that it did much good! As she reached the open door of the barn Jenna peered in praying that the dog was curled up asleep in a corner. But even in the gloom of the barn it was clear that the dog wasn't there. Slightly disappointed Jenna went about feeding the grumpy gelding his breakfast before he broke his stable door down. He was such a Diva!

With no sign of the dog, Jenna finished tending to Snow Prince and then returned to the farm house to raid the fridge for food for the dog. Grabbing a couple of cooked sausages for the dog and some fresh orange juice for herself Jenna slunk back towards the stables. As she broke the sausages into small pieces onto the tray she hoped their smell would entice the dog to appear again. Sadly though it didn't and she wondered if it was off somewhere sleeping off all the food it had eaten last night?

As she turned Snow Prince out into the paddock she wandered down to the edge of the woods, there was still no sign of the dog. Today was Friday and she was hoping that she would see the dog a few more times before the weekend as she planned to try and catch it then, with the help of Zoe. She stood silently only moving to sweep a few untamed strands of hair out of her face but still there was no sign of the dog.

Sighing she headed back towards the stables to muck out before she was due to catch the school bus but as she walked round the side of the barn there was the dog! It was eating hungrily from the tray and didn't hear Jenna approaching. Holding her breath Jenna stood stock still not knowing what to do. If she moved she would spook the dog but if she did nothing it would probably still run off. The dog soon finished its breakfast and it suddenly caught sight of Jenna standing by the barn and froze, lowering its body slightly as it prepared to run.

"It's OK, I'm not going to hurt you" Jenna whispered in a soft voice. The dogs tail started to wag slightly but Jenna knew this could be a sign of fear so she kept her voice low and her eyes on the floor so the dog didn't see her as a threat.

As she slowly moved towards the dog it started to back away, its eyes fixed firmly on Jenna. Why was it so scared? Its soft brown eyes looked so sad that Jenna just wanted to scoop it up and hold it close but she knew that with such a terrified dog she would probably get bitten first!

Feeling in her pocket Jenna's shaking fingers soon found what they were looking for and as she pulled her hand carefully out, her clenched fist unfurled to reveal two pieces of half squashed sausage. Jenna had kept a couple of bits back in case she saw the dog with the hope if using them to tempt it close.

The dog's nose twitched hungrily and it licked its lips as the smell of food reached its senses. Jenna slowly squatted down and gently rolled a piece towards the dog. The dog went to grab the food but paused, waiting for Jenna to make a grab for it but when she didn't it trotted forward and swallowed the food without chewing. With the one remaining piece still in her hand Jenna came up with a plan. Having spotted that the barn door was still open to the side of her, she carefully stood up and moved slightly away from it and the dog who was now watching her intently.

Throwing the piece of sausage through the door way Jenna held her breath. The dog, now sniffing the air rapidly, hesitated for what seemed like ages before it trotted into the barn after the sweet smelling food.

Quick as a flash Jenna ran to the door and shut it tight behind it. Shaking like a leaf she quickly checked her watch. She only had 20 minutes left before the bus came! Wedging the door shut with a pile of bricks Jenna ran flat out to the house praying that no one was in the kitchen. Thankfully no one was and as she raided the last of the cooked sausages from the fridge she stuffed them in her pocket and ran back to the barn.

Peering into the darkness of the barn Jenna could tell the dog was still in there as it let out a deep growl from the far back corner.

"Good baby" she whispered and dropped the sausages in through the gap before re-shutting and blocking up the door once again.

With a pounding heart she jogged back towards the house, this time her mum stood stirring a pot of tea in the kitchen as she staggered through the door trying to look unflustered!

"All OK?" Her mum asked as Jenna tried to act as normal as possible.

"Yep all good thanks" Jenna grinned "I'm just running a bit late" she continued as she shot through the kitchen and up the stairs to get changed. She couldn't wait to get on the school bus and tell Zoe what she had done!

CHAPTER 5

The bus ride to school had gone so quickly and as a stunned Zoe listened opened-mouthed to Jenna's excitedly told story of her adventure with the dog she struggled to take it all in,

"Slow down, slow down..." Zoe had hissed at her crazy friend as she tried to keep Jenna still and quiet enough in her seat before half the bus found out about the dog!

"So you're telling me that there's been this strange dog wandering around your farm for two days and you have managed to trap it in the barn with a sausage?" Zoe giggled as Jenna tried to calm her excitement.

"Yes, yes" beamed Jenna, as she took a quick

look around the bus to make sure no one else was listening.

"The poor thing is so scared and so hungry and I couldn't just leave it to wander off somewhere else and..."

"Whoa, whoa, whhhooooaaaa.." Zoe interrupted quickly not quite believing what she was hearing.

"So where is this dog now?" She quizzed. "Not still in the barn?"

Jenna who had slightly calmed down at this point nodded eagerly

"Yep, it's still in the barn" she beamed looking rather pleased with herself,

"and what are you going to do with a terrified dog that's trapped in the barn....?" Zoe continued.

Jenna's grin suddenly vanished, she hadn't thought about what she would do next. Everything had happened so quickly that it had completely slipped her mind!

"Uuuummmm, well, when we get back from school we can go down and see if we can get a lead on it?" Jenna smiled awkwardly at her friend.

"And what if the dog isn't friendly and we both get bitten?" Zoe questioned.

"I'm sure it's more frightened than vicious" Jenna assured her "Once it learns that we're friendly I'm sure we can easily get a lead on it." She nodded. Zoe wasn't so sure...

Throughout all their classes the girls had been somewhat distracted and although Zoe tried not to show it she too was just as excited as Jenna about there being a mystery dog in the barn. Who did it belong to? And how had it got on the farm? Why was it so afraid? All these questions she was sure would be answered if they could get hold of the dog as it was sure to be wearing a collar and tag?

As they sat together on the journey home the girls put a plan together as to what they would do about catching the dog.

"What happens if your parents or Ed have been down to the barn whilst you've been at school?" Zoe suddenly asked. That had also not crossed Jenna's mind and as they both got off the bus outside High Forest Farm they planned what to say if they walked in and got questioned about there being a crazy dog living in the barn!

Opening the front door whilst trying to act totally normal and unflustered, the girls were very relieved to find Jenna's mum curled up on the sofa chatting to Ed about a trip to Paris he had planned with some friends. After making polite conversation about their day both girls shot upstairs to change into some scruffy clothes. Luckily Zoe and Jenna were the same size so borrowing clothes was not a problem for Zoe.

Sneaking out half a loaf of bread and some of Betsy's dog biscuits the girls scurried down to the barn with fingers crossed that the dog hadn't escaped. On reaching the doors Jenna felt a wash of relief as she spotted the bricks wedging the door shut still in place.

Deciding to first peer in through a gap in the wood to see if they could spot the dog the girls quietly gazed in. The barn was so dark inside that it was hard to make out anything and it was only when Zoe knocked over a piece of wood which had been lent against the wall that they heard a noise from inside. "It's still in there" beamed Jenna. But they still had a dilemma, how would they get into the barn and not let the dog rush out? Jenna had luckily bought a torch down with her as she knew how gloomy the barn was especially as it would soon start to get dark outside.

Opening the creaking door slowly Jenna switched on the torch and began to peer round the edge of the door hoping that the dog would just be sat there wagging its tail, but there was no sign of it.

"We are going to have to go in" Zoe whispered, trying to keep the fear out of her voice.

As both of the girls squeezed in through the gap in the door they stood quietly in the shadowy barn as Jenna shone the torch slowly round looking for any sign of the dog. The barn wasn't that big but with piles of dusty wood littering the floor there were plenty of places where the dog could hide.

Both the girls could feel their hearts pounding in their chests and as they neared the back of the barn they heard a rustling in the left hand corner followed by a deep growl.

Zoe, not wanting to stay in the dark with a growling, frightened dog, spun on her heels and headed back for the door but Jenna quick as a flash grabbed her wrist.

"Just wait" she whispered.

Zoe nodded, too scared to speak. Jenna released her grip and carefully opened up the bag of bread and dog biscuits and with a smooth flick threw a few in the direction on the growling. As the food landed the growling stopped and Jenna held her breath as a scruffy shape dragged itself on its belly towards the food. The poor dog was terrified

Crouching down Jenna gently clicked her tongue and held out a piece of bread from a quivering hand. "Come on sweetie" she whispered her voice trembling. The dog's stumpy tail began to wag slightly and Jenna knew her voice was helping to calm the dog.

"Good dog, that's it" she soothed as the dog inched closer.

As the dog's nose reached her outstretched hand Jenna worried it would grab the bread from her but instead the dog carefully took the bread and backed slowly away, back to the corner from where it had been hidden. Zoe, now feeling braver, crouched on the floor alongside her friend and gave Jenna a quick reassuring smile. The dog soon reappeared and this time its tail was wagging harder.

Holding out a few biscuits Jenna made the dog come a little before she let it take one and then when she felt it was safe to do so she gently stroked the dog's head as it ate.

"You poor thing, why are you so scared?" she gently questioned the dog. It just looked up at her with huge black eyes.

As she smoothed its trembling neck she was disappointed to find it didn't have a collar on. The dog ate the remaining biscuits within a flash leaving the girls to wonder how long it had been living wild.

Zoe had gone back outside to fetch a bowl of

water and when she returned she found Jenna sat against the barn wall with the dog lying across her lap.

"Isn't she beautiful?" Jenna beamed

"She?" Zoe looked at her friend, puzzled. Jenna nodded and revealed the dog's belly which showed a neat row of teats on an already rounded belly!

"Puppies??" Zoe stood opened mouthed. Jenna grinned

"That's what it looks like to me" she smiled, "No wonder she was so hungry, she's got babies to feed as well as herself" she sighed. "We need to get her to the vets quickly I think and see if she has a microchip and an owner."

Zoe, still a little overwhelmed by the whole situation, just stood and nodded again.

"Do well tell your parents now?" She smirked.

"I think we best" replied Jenna.

CHAPTER 6

The girls had decided that they would edit the whole dog in the barn story slightly to…

"Look what we found in the paddock Mum," as they thought that if her parents knew that she had firstly trapped a terrified dog in the barn and then fed it half the kitchen contents she might not get the reaction she hoped for.

By the time they got back into the farmhouse Jenna's parents were standing in the kitchen preparing vegetables for dinner. As soon as the girls walked in Jenna's dad immediately guessed something was up!

"Evening girls and what have we been up to?" He smiled as he looked them up and down, puzzled. Jenna quickly noticed that both she and Zoe were covered in dusty paw prints!

"We found a dog in the paddock and it was really scared and we....." As Zoe blurted out the start of a muddled story, Jenna quickly interrupted her and gave her a look that said it all.

"Yes we found a little dog in the paddock all alone so we caught it and its not got a collar on and I think it might be pregnant."

Jenna's story hadn't quite come out as she planned but she thought her parents got the picture!

"You found a dog?" Jenna's mum quickly dried her hands in a towel "Where is it now?" she asked. "It's in the barn" Jenna smiled

"Well you best bring it up for us to see I think" her mum said puzzled. "Is it friendly?" She suddenly added

"Oh yes" said Zoe "Very, she was just a bit scared to start with" Jenna shot her friend another freezing look just in case Zoe blabbed everything!

"Well let me shut Betsy in the living room and you go fetch the dog on one of her leads and we will see what we're dealing with" Jenna's dad smiled. He was just as big a softie as Jenna when it came to the animals.

The little black dog was so pleased to see the girls again and its bottom and tail wiggled so much when it saw them that it nearly fell over! She walked so well on the lead that the girls both agreed that she must have a loving home somewhere.

As they went into the kitchen the dog crouched down nervously,

"Come on girl" Jenna encouraged "It's OK". As she led the dog through the hallway to where her parents were waiting her mum immediately bent down to stroke the dog but the poor thing tore backwards quivering.

"Steady there" her mum smiled and the dog soon crept back up and sniffed and then licked her hand. "Looks like she's had a rough time?" Jenna's dad said quietly.

"Come on let's get her to the vet before they shut for the evening. "Hopefully she has a microchip and we can get her back to her rightful home." He winked.

The Vet clinic was only a short drive across Brannton and the dog sat calmly between Jenna and Zoe on the back seat enjoying the fuss she was getting. She was such a gentle and loving dog that Jenna just couldn't understand how she had ended up living wild.

As they pulled up into the big car park behind the vet's they immediately noticed a large white van parked in the far corner. Two men sat smoking in the front seats.

"Yuck, I hate smoking" Jenna whispered under her breath.

As the dog jumped out of the car after the girls, the two men in the van suddenly started talking between themselves and gesturing towards the family.

"What's up?" Jenna's dad asked as he saw her staring towards the van.

"Those men seem to recognise the dog" she whispered "But something doesn't feel right Dad" she continued. Ruffling her hair he laughed to himself. "

Come on Little Miss Suspicious, let's get her in to the surgery and see what they say," and putting an arm around her shoulders they walked across the tarmac to the entrance.

As her parents explained how they had found the dog to the receptionist, Jenna and Zoe kept a close eye on the car park to see if they could see any more of the men or the white van.

"They might just be delivery people?" Zoe shrugged.

"I don't know, something just seemed odd to me

about how they acted when they saw the dog" Jenna replied.

As they found a seat in the mostly empty waiting room the little dog continued to lick Jenna's hand nervously. Within a few minutes a kindly looking lady vet with a high pony tail asked them to come through to the consulting room.

Jenna explained herself this time how she had found the dog in the field looking lost and frightened and how it hadn't been wearing a name tag or collar.

"We also think she's having puppies" Zoe added excitedly. The vet smiled warmly and asked Jenna's dad to lift the dog carefully onto the table so she could have a proper look at her.

Checking the dog's eyes and teeth first and then listening to her heart and breathing the vet commented that despite being, dirty, smelly and a bit underweight the dog was in a healthy condition. As she felt the dogs rounded stomach she grinned at the girls.

"There are definitely puppies in there! And I should think she is only a few days away from having them as she already has a lot of milk there as well" she nodded. "You did a great job bringing her here, especially in her condition.

Let's see if we can find her owner" and as she left the room to find the microchip scanner the girls beamed excitedly at each other and cuddled the dog.

As the vet came back in she gently stroked the dogs neck and as she ran the scanner over the area the microchip would be implanted there was a loud beep.

"There we go" she winked at the girls, she has been chipped so give me a minute and I will check the number against the database and see if we can contact her owner.

"Well that was worth the trip, wasn't it?" Jenna's dad smiled. "She is a lovely little dog, someone must be really missing her".

After what seemed like ages the vet came back in.

"Well the good news is we have her logged on the database but the phone number of her owners isn't working anymore". "This does happen sometimes as owners change phones or addresses and don't think to update the microchip records". She frowned.

"So what do we do now" Jenna asked nervously. "I don't want her going into a cold kennels somewhere". The vet told them that by law she had to report the dog to the Dog Warden and again she left the room to make a phone call.

"Why would you not think to update your dog's details?" Jenna muttered crossly. Karen, Jenna's mother, suddenly thought of something.

"Did we update Betsy's records when we moved here?" she asked Jenna.

"Oh" Jenna replied, "no I don't think we did Mum," she replied a little embarrassed, "but tomorrow I'm doing it first thing before school" she nodded eagerly.

As the vet returned she didn't look very happy

"I've just spoken to Claire the local Dog Warden and she says that their kennels are full and she can't take the dog for a few days. Are you able to take care of the dog for a bit longer?" she asked the family hopefully.

"If I say 'no' my life wouldn't be worth living" Jenna's dad laughed. "Yes of course we can" he nodded happily.

The vet wrote down the microchip number for them and advised that they perhaps contact a few Rescue centres to ask around about anyone losing a dog in the area. She also mentioned that the dog had been registered to an address a fair way away and she had a suspicion that the dog could turn out to be stolen.

"Stolen?" Zoe spluttered, not quite believing what she was hearing.

"I'm afraid there has been a huge problem across the whole country of family pets being stolen to be used for breeding on puppy farms and sold on to unsuspecting people" the vet said sadly shaking her head. "It's an awful business" The girls looked at each other with horror, neither of them had had any clue that dog theft was such a huge problem.

CHAPTER 7

As they left the vet's surgery with the little black dog trotting happily along at their heels Jenna wondered what would happen if they couldn't find the dog's owners. Would they be able to keep her? She best not ask her parents that yet as she was sure the answer would be 'NO!'

Crossing the darkly lit car park Jenna kept her eyes on the white van that was still parked in the corner. This time there didn't appear to be any one with it and she felt slightly relieved. Perhaps they had just been workmen sitting having a coffee? She couldn't help finding the men suspicious as they had seemed so interested in the dog, but for what reason? Trying to push the thoughts out of her mind they climbed into the back seat of the car and headed for home.

As her dad turned the car onto the main road Jenna looked back to the car park one more time, she wasn't sure why but as she did she noticed that the white van now had its head lights on and was also leaving the car park. As it turned onto the same road as them Jenna felt her heart start to beat a little faster, she was sure she was just being silly but something was telling her that something just wasn't right!

Zoe had noticed that her friend was looking worried so she tapped Jenna on the knee and whispered "What's up?" Jenna sat silently staring at her, should she say something or would Zoe think she was mad? Keeping her voice to a whisper so her parents didn't hear her Jenna lent over to her friend.

"I'm worried that van is following us,"

"Following us?" Zoe whispered back, Jenna nodded

"There's just something odd about the men in it, I'm not sure what but I've just got a bad feeling about them." She continued biting her lip.

Zoe turned round in her seat to have a look but Jenna thumped her in the arm

"Don't make it so obvious" she hissed.

"OK chill out!" Zoe hissed back "I'm sure they are just heading the same way as us". The van continued to follow them all the way back to High Forest Farm but instead of following them down the drive it slowed slightly and then continued straight on, much to the girls relief!

"See, I told you" Zoe smirked smugly. Jenna just stuck her tongue out at her friend and they both laughed.

Finding an old duvet Jenna's mum made the dog a temporary bed by the Aga,

"We will need to find her a proper whelping box" she sighed "Just in case she is still with us when she has her puppies."

Both Jenna and Zoe were so excited at the thought of puppies that they almost forgot that this wasn't their dog and that somewhere her real owner was desperate to find her.

After dinner the girls headed upstairs to use Jenna's laptop to search the Internet for possible lost dogs. The vet had said that the little dog was a Spaniel so the girls started their search there. Within seconds hundreds of pages came up all linked to missing dogs.

"No way!" Zoe sighed, "There are hundreds, the vet was right about there being such a big problem". Jenna sat silently staring at the screen. She felt so saddened by this whole stolen dog business that she didn't really want to believe any of it but here it was, as clear as day on her computer screen.

One of the first sites that popped up was called 'Dog Lost', it was a site dedicated to listing those dogs reported stolen/missing and also found. It including locations they had been lost from and photos. The photos often pictured the missing dogs being cuddled by their families and this gave Jenna chills, how could people steal other people's pets?

"Right, come on let's make a start!" Jenna sighed as she scanned the endless pages of photos, there were so many dogs of all breeds ages and colours, but they had to start somewhere.

Using the search feature on the page the girls looked specifically for spaniels and as they clicked search a long list of possible dogs appeared.

"What if this dog has been missing a while?" questioned Zoe, "Would the owners just give up all hope and stop searching?" Spinning round in her seat to look her friend straight in the eyes Jenna just simply said

"Would you stop looking and hoping if it was your dog?" Zoe shook her head quickly

"No way, I could never give up" she replied.

After an hour of searching the girls had found a few dogs matching the description and had decided that they needed to get some good photos of the dog and upload them onto the site. Hopefully the owner would check the Dog Lost site daily and would recognise their dog.

As they skipped down the stairs Jenna spotted the dog led upside down in her temporary bed with her legs stuck in the air, her swollen puppy filled belly looking twice the size it had earlier.

"Well someone looks at home" she giggled.

CHAPTER 8

J enna had taken some great shots of the dog on her camera and Zoe had made a list of the dog's markings on a note pad, they had done all they could to get an accurate description of her and now they just needed to get it on the website and see what happened. Jenna's dad had warned about making posters of the dog as he was worried that people would try and claim the dog was theirs, especially as she was due to have puppies.

It was easy enough to add the dog to the website and they hoped that by the morning the poor owner would have recognised the dog and got in contact. Clipping Betsy's lead on to the little black dog's collar the girls led her into the garden and down to the paddock to see if she needed the toilet.

As they waited shivering in the cold they spotted headlights heading down the drive.

"That should be my dad coming to collect me." Zoe said rubbing her frozen hands together in an attempt to warm them up.

"Let's take this one up to meet them" Jenna suggested and they wandered back up towards the front of the house.

As they came alongside the house they heard voices, but not voices they recognised.

"Who's that?" Zoe asked her teeth chattering from the cold. Jenna put her finger to her lips in a signal for Zoe to be quiet while she listened to the conversation between her dad and the visitors.

As they peered around the edge of the house the girls spotted a large white van.

"It's the men from the car park" hissed a worried Jenna.

"What are they doing here?" Zoe hissed back.

"I don't know, but I don't think it's good" Jenna worried, biting her lip.

As the girls listened they could hear Jenna's dad telling the men politely but firmly that he didn't need any more firewood and would they kindly leave his property. Jenna didn't believe the men were here to sell firewood because as her dad shut the front door she spotted a third man heading back to the van from the other side of the house. What was he up to? Deciding to go in through the back door the girls quickly found Jenna's dad and told him about the third man.

"I knew there was something odd about them" Jenna's dad tutted shaking his head.

"I think they were checking the farm out for something to steal Dad" Jenna worried. With that there was another knock at the door but this time much to all their relief it was Brian, Zoe's dad.

"Did you pass a white van on the lane?" Jenna asked him.

"I did indeed" Brian replied " There have been a few incidents in the village of locks being cut off and property being stolen, so I took down the registration number" he nodded.

"Nice work Dad" smiled Zoe. Brian winked back at her and Jenna told him what had happened with the other man checking out the farm whilst the other two men kept her dad talking.

"Can I borrow your house phone please as I want to report it to the local Police straight away?" He asked.

"It might be nothing but I think it definitely wants reporting". The girls looked at each other, "we need to check on Snow Prince" Jenna announced but as she went to grab a torch her dad stopped her.

"I will come down with you in a minute" he assured her. "Those men might still be about so I don't want you going out there alone. Let's ring the Police and see what they say then we will go down and check on Snow Prince." Jenna thought about arguing but she was actually a bit relieved that she wouldn't have to walk to the stables alone.

Because Jenna's dad had seen and spoken to the men it was decided that it was best for him to ring the police and while he was giving them the details the girls showed Brian the dog. As he bent down to fuss the dog the poor thing quivered and shook.

"Why is she so nervous?" he asked as he gently scratched the dog's head to gain her confidence,

"She's been living wild for a few days" Jenna explained

"The vet thinks she could be possibly stolen" she sighed. "She is microchipped but the phone number on the database isn't working, so where she's come from is a bit of a mystery".

Brian shook his head in disbelief,

"I had read in the papers that there has been a

rise in the number of dogs being stolen" he said glumly.

"Puppies can be worth anywhere from £300 to £600 and with a dog having anywhere from 3 to 7 puppies that's a lot of money to be made, although sadly the welfare of the dogs used for breeding is far from good, they are just puppy making machines"

"Wow" exclaimed Zoe "I never knew that puppies cost so much!"

Now I know why horrible people steal them!" Jenna too was shocked at how much money could be made by stealing a dog.

"Rescue centres are full of puppies and dogs needing homes so why do people buy from these Puppy Farms?" she said crossly.

"Probably because these Puppy farms put up cute photos of puppies and don't care who they sell them to so anyone can buy them" Brian explained.

As Jenna's dad finished his call he informed them all that the registration number on the white van was fake and the Police were passing on the details to the patrol cars in the area to see if they could catch up with it.

"Another mystery then!?" joked Brian.

After checking Snow Prince was still present and correct Jenna and her dad checked the rest of the buildings and sheds near the house, which thankfully were all undisturbed. The frosty night air soon made them head in for the night and after one last shine of the torch up the dark driveway they headed back into the warmth of the house.

Jenna had always been a whizz on the computer and it didn't take her long to figure out how to upload the photos and description onto the Dog Lost website and as she clicked the upload button she hoped that by the morning she would have a response from the dog's real owner.

CHAPTER 9

After a rather restless night's sleep which had been filled with dreams of scared dogs locked in cold barns, Jenna awoke and sat rubbing the sleep from her eyes as the pale winter sun filtered through the gap in her curtains. She immediately remembered she needed to check her emails for any responses to the photos she had put up of the dog. As the computer whirred into life, Jenna peered out of her bedroom window across to the stables and was relieved to see Snow Prince scratching his nose on the top of his stable door. Settling back on to her bedroom chair Jenna blinked at the brightness of the laptop screen.

"You have 5 new Emails"

"Yesss..." She squeaked excitedly and clicked on her mail box. 5 new messages, this sounded hopeful!

The first two messages were just spam ones so she quickly deleted them but the next three were all responses from the Dog Lost website. Feeling her heart rate quicken Jenna opened and started to read the first one. It was from a lady in Scotland who had lost her spaniel three months ago whilst out for a walk and although she was sure that the dog Jenna was caring for wasn't hers she wanted to double check that it didn't have a white tip to its tail. Putting her dressing gown on and ramming her feet into her tatty sippers Jenna headed down to the kitchen to check the dog's tail. The little black dog had heard her coming and greeted her at the foot of the stairs with a wagging stumpy tail and despite the wagging Jenna could tell that the tail was most definitely all black!

"Come on Little Miss Mystery" she smiled at the dog, let's see if you need the toilet. As she let Betsy out of the living room the two dogs spent a minute sniffing each other with great interest before Jenna let them out onto the frosty lawn.

"Please don't run off" Jenna begged but she had no need to worry, the dog stuck to Betsy like glue as the trotted about the lawn to do their business and then dived back in when Jenna rattled the treat tin.

Leaving the dogs happily snacking, Jenna

sprinted back up the stairs to read the remaining emails and reply to one asking about the dog's tail. The next two emails were from the same email address and both emails were identical making Jenna think that they were sent by someone with nervous fingers!

It was from another lady and this time it mentioned that her friend had lost a dog two years ago after it was stolen from her back garden. As Jenna read on the email explained that the lady's friend was away on holiday and that she was desperately trying to get hold of her as she said the dog Jenna had found looked very similar to the missing one, even down to the small white splodge on its chin!

Jenna emailed back straight away asking for any photos the woman may have so they could compare and asked if she also had access to the dog microchip number. Realising the time, Jenna panicked slightly and threw on her old clothes before running out the house to see to Snow Prince.

With her chores done in super-fast time she grabbed some fruit for breakfast before almost crashing into her mum as they met on the stairs. After explaining to her mum about the e-mail she had received, Jenna's mum promised she would keep a close eye on the little dog and the emails while Jenna was at school. Changing into her uniform at record speed Jenna spent her last few minutes making a fuss of the little dog,

"We will soon get you home" she whispered and with a last look over her shoulder she disappeared out of the front door and headed for the bus stop. She couldn't wait to tell Zoe that they had already had a possible home for the dog. She knew Zoe would be as excited as her and although it might not be the same dog it was a good start to getting the dog back to its rightful owner.

The girls chatted excitedly the whole way to school and although the day did drag in the usual same way they soon were chatting again on the journey home. As the bus wound its way through the country lanes Jenna spotted something that made her heart skip a beat. It was the white van that had visited the farm last night, this time it was parked in the car park of The Red Fox pub.

"What do we do?" whispered a nervous Zoe as her breath steamed up the cold bus window.

"We need to get the registration number, quick!" Jenna whispered back and quickly wrote the number on the misted up glass before rummaging in her bag for a pen and paper.

"You should work for the Police!" giggled Zoe, amazed at her friend's quick thinking.

As the bus finally pulled in to let the girls off at the top of the Farm's drive the girls raced in to find Jenna's dad only to find he wasn't back from work yet.

"I've got a plan" Jenna grinned with a glint in her eye

"What...?" asked Zoe looking nervously at her friend, she was still getting used to Jenna and her slightly mad ideas!

"Let's go to the Red Fox and see if we can find out any more about those men and the van" Jenna suggested with a determined look in her eye.

"Are you totally crazy??" Zoe squeaked "They could be dangerous!" Jenna just laughed even more "We aren't going to go grab hold of them!! "Just wander past and see what we can see." "I've been meaning to visit Victoria for the last week or so, so why not?" Jenna smirked.

CHAPTER 10

After a quick change of clothes the girls left a note to say that they were going to visit Victoria and hurriedly left for The Red Fox. They had thought about taking the dogs with them but Jenna felt it was too far for the Little Black dog so after a quick run in the garden she left them in the warm of the house.

"The van might not even be there?" Zoe suggested to her friend as they marched along the pavement. "But it might be!" grinned back Jenna. "If it isn't then we can just chat to Victoria and tell her about the dog", Jenna always thought one step ahead and that reassured Zoe, although she still wasn't 100% sure she wanted to go and spy on possible criminals!

As they neared the car park of the pub Jenna

stopped dead, causing Zoe who was struggling to keep up with her to crash into her back.

"It's still there!" Jenna whispered. Now it was her that was doubting whether this was such a good idea. As they crossed the tarmac they noticed that no-one was in the van and without looking too obvious, Jenna snapped a photo of it on her phone.

"Where do you think the men are?" Zoe asked nervously.

"Probably in there" Jenna replied, nodding towards the Red Fox. "Let's go find Victoria, she might know who they are?"

As they pushed open the heavy wood and glass door the girls felt a rush of relief as the spotted Victoria writing on the chalk menu board by the bar. She had her long light brown hair piled high on her head in a messy bun which despite the description looked like it had been done by a hairdresser! Jenna had always admired how Victoria dressed as it looked smart yet effortless.

Turning to look towards the door Victoria quickly spotted the girls and her face lit up with a beaming smile.

"Hey you two! What brings you here?" she called warmly. With Zoe nervously looking around the bar area it didn't take a mind reader to notice that something was up.

"Let me get you a lemonade each and we can have a catch up over there," Victoria winked and putting down her chalkboard she grabbed some glasses from behind the bar. The girls made their way over to where Victoria had pointed and as they headed for the seats they noticed a group of men sat in the corner by the toilet doors.

Catching each other's eyes Jenna grabbed Zoe's arm and guided her to an empty seat before her friend made her staring too obvious.

"That's them" hissed Zoe

"I know!" Jenna whispered back. With that Victoria arrived with the drinks and picked up on the girls nervous faces

"OK you two, spill the beans" and as she sat down on one of the red cushioned seats Jenna started to tell her the whole story of the dog.

Victoria listened intently to what she was being told and when Jenna got to the part about the men in the van coming to the farm her face dropped.

"I knew there was something about those three" she replied in a low voice. "They've been in here off and on for the last day or so and spend a lot of time making whispering phone calls." "I have chatted to them a couple of times when I served their drinks but all they are interested in is making a fuss of Plumb."

'Plumb' was Victoria's little tan and white terrier who had her bed behind the bar whilst Victoria worked. She had re-homed her from a customer whose job involved long hours forcing them to leave Plumb home alone a lot of the time.

With that the little terrier trotted out from behind the bar, wagging it's stumpy little tail as it sniffed it's way round the table and chair legs looking for dropped scraps of food. As she wandered past the table where the three men sat one of the men bent down and scooped her up on to his lap.

"Victoria look!" Jenna whispered as she nudged her arm. "Why have they picked her up?" Victoria stood up from where she was sitting and walked over to collect Plumb from the men.

"Such a sweet little dog" said one of the men who was wearing a dark blue stripe top

"Do you want to come home with me?" he joked, holding Plumb up in front of him. Victoria carefully took hold of the little dog and smiled politely at the men.

"No chance, she's all mine," she winked and marched back to the table to sit with the girls.

"I don't trust those guys" Jenna murmured under her breath to Victoria.

"Me neither" sighed Victoria.

As Jenna, Zoe and Victoria all chatted away about what they had all been up to over the last week or so Jenna couldn't help but keep half an eye on the three men. As the men sat drinking one of their mobile phones started to ring loudly and one of the men wearing a heavy black coat answered it quickly and kept his voice low and quiet as he chatted to the caller. The two remaining men stopped talking and listened intently to the conversation and obviously hearing something they liked the two men rubbed their hands together and started to laugh. Jenna couldn't just sit and watch anymore and after making the excuse of needing the toilet left Victoria and Zoe talking and headed to the Ladies toilet door next to wear the men were sat.

As she passed their table she strained to hear what the men were saying but the man on the phone caught her eye for a second, making Jenna blush slightly as if she had been caught spying. As she pushed the toilet's white painted door open

Jenna heard one of the men clearly say in a gruff voice

"He's gunna bring them to the car park in a bit". Who was 'they'? Jenna had to find out more as she had this nagging feeling that these men were up to no good again!

Shutting the door behind her and checking she was alone in the toilets, Jenna went back to the door and, pressing her ear up against it, listened carefully. All she could hear to start with was muffled voices but as she listened more she started to hear what the men were saying more clearly.

"Tell him to park right by the side of our van. We don't want another one escaping." Escaping?? Jenna felt the hairs on her neck stand up and a cold shiver ran through her body. She had an awful feeling she now knew what they were talking about!

"And make sure you keep them quiet as well, we don't want the barking catching people's attention" the man continued before ending the call. Jenna stood frozen at the door it was now confirmed in her mind. These men were dog thieves!

Hearing footsteps heading her way Jenna ran to the nearest toilet and flushed it, then trying to look composed she started to wash her hands in the sink.

As the creaking door opened Jenna felt a rush of relief as Zoe walked in humming to herself.

"We wondered where you had got to?" Laughed Zoe but one look at Jenna's pale face told her to something was very wrong.

"What is it?" Zoe asked quietly, now worried about why her usually fearless friend looked so shaken.

"It's those men" Jenna murmured her voice breaking slightly.

"What about them...? Zoe asked, slightly nervous as to what the answer would be!

"They're dog thieves!" Jenna stuttered.

"Dog thieves? Jenna how do you know that?" Zoe hissed trying to keep her voice quiet.

As Jenna explained what she had overheard Zoe stood open mouthed.

"What do we do?" She gasped holding her face in her hands. Jenna knew exactly what they should do,

"We need to speak to Victoria, she will know what to do".

CHAPTER 11

Not knowing how long they had before the people the man had been talking to arrived, Jenna and Zoe made their way calmly back to the table where Victoria was sitting nursing Plumb on her lap.

"Oh there you are" she beamed as the girls sat down, "I was just about to send out a search party for you two!" she laughed. But seeing the girls worried faces she knew something serious was up and as Jenna told her what she had heard Victoria knew that her suspicions about the men had been correct.

"What do we do now?" Jenna asked tentatively,

"I don't know as we haven't got any evidence apart from what you heard," Victoria replied sadly. "If I ring the police they will only log the call and probably won't send an Officer out straight away" . Jenna thought for a second and then quickly said, "Well let's get some evidence then..."

Victoria immediately shook her head but then as she looked up at Jenna's face she knew that this was one girl who wouldn't take no for an answer!

"And what do you intend to do then?" Victoria asked, not really wanting to hear what Jenna had planned. "You don't even know if these guys are dog thieves!" "And if you think you can just go following them outside to see what they get up to, think again, it's far too dangerous."

Jenna sat quietly staring at the floor, her long straight hair falling loosely over her face,

"I know what I heard" she muttered, "They are awaiting some of their horrid friends who have been out stealing peoples pets! I'm not going to sit here and let them drive away into the night" .

Victoria reached out a gentle hand and carefully brushed Jenna's hair from her face.

"Look, I'm going to go call the police and tell them our suspicions", "You two sit here and don't do anything stupid, promise?" She told the girls firmly. Zoe nodded but Jenna just stared at the floor and drummed her fingers in annoyance on the wooden table. As Victoria left to ring the police,

Jenna sat upright and looked over towards the men who were finishing up their drinks and laughing between themselves.

"I'm going to go ring my parents" she told Zoe with a half-smile, "they will wonder why I've been so long.".Zoe who still looked half terrified, nodded glumly

"OK but please don't be long, I don't want to sit here by myself."

As Jenna made her way outside she fumbled with a shaking hand into her pocket for her phone, she wasn't sure if her hands were shaking with cold, anger or both. Surely the police would come and investigate the van? Dog theft was a serious crime wasn't it?

Before she could press any buttons her phone started to ring, its screen illuminating as it demanded to be answered.

Hello?" Jenna answered in a puzzled voice,

"Jenna? It's Mum, are you OK? Hello?"

Jenna was a bit taken aback that the person she was about to ring had just called her.

"Hi Mum, yeah I'm fine" "I was just about to ring you, I left a note and..." but before Jenna could continue her mum cut her off mid-sentence.

"Jenna just listen to me for a second. Have you

got the dogs with you?" Her mum's words chilled Jenna to the core.

"No why? What's wrong?" Asked Jenna, as her heart beat faster and faster.

"We've had a break in at home and we can't find either of the dogs. The back door has been smashed open, there's glass everywhere," Karen continued, her voice trembling as she explained what she had found after returning home. Jenna managed to compose herself enough to tell her mum that she didn't have the dogs before bursting into tears. As huge fat tears poured down her face, Jenna struggled to speak and as she turned around to go and find Victoria, the phone slipped from her frozen fingers, as it hit the black glittering tarmac it shattered into pieces.

"Nooooo" Jenna scrabbled in the dark trying to find the various pieces but it was pointless. Leaving the bits of phone sparkling in the moonlight, she raced back into the pub trying to dry her tear-stained eyes on her jacket as she went. Zoe spotted her immediately and leapt to her feet and as she got to her friend Jenna grabbed her arm and dragged her outside.

"What is it? What's happened?" Zoe begged her sobbing friend

"There's been a break in at the farm" Jenna sobbed, "They've taken the dogs!" Zoe stood stunned, did she hear right?

"Who's taken the dogs? Jenna, who has taken the dogs?" She hissed at her friend as she got hold of Jenna's trembling shoulders.

"I don't know" Jenna spluttered trying to get herself together. "Mum rang and asked if we had the dogs with us as there has been a break in at home. I said 'no' and then I stupidly dropped my phone and it broke. We need to get Victoria and tell her what's happened".

As the girls headed back into the pub they were met by the three men walking out and as the man in the black jacket passed them he winked. Jenna was incensed but before she could say anything Zoe dragged her back out to the car park.

"It's them Zoe, it's them and their nasty friends. They've got the dogs I know it!" she wailed as Zoe tried to calm her down and keep her quiet.

"You don't know that Jenna, but if they have got something to do with it then we need to find out where they are going?" Zoe continued as she still tried in vain to calm Jenna down.

The man in the black jacket had headed to the van which was parked at the back of the car park as the two remaining men lit cigarettes and wandered across to the edge of the road, obviously on the look-out for their friends. Jenna noticed through her tear stained eyes that the man in the black jacket was patting his coat pockets and peering on the ground around him.

"He's left his keys inside! Zoe, he's left his keys inside!" Jenna suddenly had an idea and she prayed she was right. Diving back in through the door Jenna told Zoe to find Victoria and tell her what had happened as she headed quickly for the men's table. Sure enough there on the table were a set of keys and without a moment's hesitation Jenna shot past the table scooping them up as she went.

CHAPTER 12

Pushing open the toilet door and shutting it quickly behind her Jenna hoped she hadn't been seen.

As she listened carefully behind the door, she heard heavy footsteps approaching and the clattering of glasses as the man in the black coat searched for his keys. After a bit of mumbling to himself and tutting Jenna heard his footsteps fade as he headed outside again. Opening the door an inch Jenna saw the coast was clear and, trying to look relaxed she headed back towards the bar to find Zoe and Victoria.

There was no sign of either of them! Thinking they must be outside Jenna headed for the door to the car park and as she felt the freezing air on her face a hand grabbed her arm. Jumping out of her skin Jenna spun round and felt a rush of relief she realised it was Victoria.

"I told you two to stay put!" she tutted under her breath.

"I know" said Jenna "Sorry!"

Victoria just shook her head and started to explain that she had rung the police and given the registration of the van the men were driving and that they did have a patrol car in the area which they were sending over to investigate.

"We just need to hope that they don't disappear when their mates turn up" she shivered.

"They won't get far without these" Jenna scowled as she opened up her hand to reveal the gleaming keys. "Jenna! Where on earth..." Victoria gasped.

"He left them on the table" Jenna explained her eyes flashing with anger.

"Zoe you never said that was what Jenna was up to!" Victoria tutted and she shook her head in disbelief at the determination of two young girls.

"I'm so sorry about the dogs, let's just hope these scum bags are responsible and we can find them safe and well. Have your parents called the police?" Victoria asked, knowing full well they would have.

"I don't know, I think so" Jenna shuddered, she couldn't stop thinking of the dogs being scared as the door got smashed open, where were they now?

As bright headlights turned into the car park Jenna prayed it was the police but as a large blue rusted van pulled up next to the men's van she knew she wouldn't be that lucky.

"That's them" hissed Zoe "It's the people that man was talking to on the phone!" "What do we do now?" Zoe pleaded to Victoria.

"Just stay still and quiet" Victoria told her. "We still don't know if they are involved with the break in at the farm or if the dogs have just escaped." Jenna just looked deep into Victoria's eyes

"It's them I know it."

As they watched two dark clothed men jumped out of the old blue van and were met by the other three men who had by now begun searching the car park floor with the light from their mobile phones.

"So what do we do now?" Zoe whispered, her teeth chattering with the cold.

"Just stay still and quiet" Victoria answered. "I'm just hoping that without any keys they won't be able to drive off and by the time they've sorted something out the police will be here".

"Where are they?" Hissed Jenna, she was

holding the keys so tightly that they were digging into her hand but she wasn't letting go of them that was for sure! As the three of them stood in the shadows with their backs against the wall they all became aware of a noise drifting across the car park from inside the blue van. The noise was familiar to them all and it was one they couldn't mistake.

"That's a dog barking!" Jenna cried angrily and as she went to run to the van a quick thinking Victoria grabbed her arm.

"Jenna please!" she pleaded "If we go charging over there accusing them of dog theft they will just drive off with possibly whatever dog's they might or might not have stolen in the back!" Jenna knew Victoria was right but the urge to run to the van and pull the doors open was almost overwhelming.

Just then one of the men wearing a baseball cap walked over to the blue van and banged on the side with his fist. The barking stopped for a second but then started again this time more frantic. Laughing to himself he whistled to the other men that were still searching the car park and they all gathered at the back of the van.

After the man in the baseball cap had fetched a torch from front of the vehicle he yanked open the heavy double doors at the back. Jenna and Zoe held their breath as they watched the space inside illumi-nate in the light of the torch beam.

"I can't see what's inside" Zoe whined, "Can you guys see anything?" Jenna couldn't answer as her throat had all but closed up and if she tried to talk she wasn't sure what would come out. Hot tears had begun to flow down her cheeks, she had never felt so helpless.

As then men laughed and pointed into the back of the van one of them climbed inside and then reappeared with something in his arms. He was struggling to hold whatever it was and as he stepped out into the moonlight it was clear what he was holding was a small white scruffy dog. "Betsy!" Jenna half yelled as Zoe swiftly put her hand over her friend's mouth, despite the fact that she too wanted to yell at the top of her voice. Before any of them could say another word, the little dog wrig-gled and squirmed so much that the man holding her put her quickly onto the floor. As they watched the little dog pulled and leapt around on the lead she was held on and within a couple of seconds had slipped the lead and bolted off.

Jenna could take no more and bolted across the car park after her.

"Jenna wait!!" Victoria screamed as she watched

in horror as the both of them headed towards the now busy road. The men spun round as they heard Jenna coming and then quickly slammed the back doors of the van shut. As Betsy reached the edge of the road a car's headlights lit up her scruffy little body and as she became frozen in the bright lights a screeching of brakes could be heard. Thankfully the quick witted terrier managed to dodge to the side of the vehicle and vanished into the dark. Jenna who had been close behind her ended up running into the front of the now stationary car much to the shock of its occupants, two police officers! Pushing herself off the patrol car, Jenna spun round to look for Betsy but there was no sign. Victoria was close behind Jenna and as she grabbed her arm again the two officers positioned the patrol car in the entrance of the car park.

"Hello girls, what's been happening here then?" One of them asked gruffly as he pulled on a reflective padded jacket.

As Victoria quickly explained what was going on, Jenna and Zoe pleaded with them to check the van. Which now had its engine running.

"OK, OK calm down ladies. Let us do our job please." He told them all firmly. As he used his radio to check out the blue van's registration the other officer went to speak to the men sat in the front. As the engine went quiet Jenna felt slightly relieved but was still desperate to find where Betsy had gone and started to call the dog's name as she frantically looked down the road in the direction she had run off in.

The crackling of a police radio caused Jenna to stop her calling for a second and as she heard the older officer ask for some back up she looked at Victoria for some reassurance.

"Why do they need back up?" Zoe asked nervously.

"I'm not sure but they've obviously found something they aren't happy about" Victoria replied.

The older officer headed back towards the blue van and asked the men to open the back doors which they did reluctantly. Victoria and the girls crept over to get a look at what was happening and as one of the officers shone a torch round the van they heard raised voices. Jenna was desperate to see if the black spaniel she had found was in their too, the poor dog was heavily pregnant and should be being looked after not thrown into the back of a rusted van in the dark.

"Are these your dogs?" The younger officer asked the group of men who were now looking very nervous. "We found them running up the road," replied the man in the baseball cap.

"Yes of course you did...!" said the Officer shaking his head. "Can you identify these dogs? The officer called to Victoria as the girls got closer.

"I can't, but this young lady can" Victoria nodded pointing to Jenna. As the girls reached the van's open doors they peered in not knowing what they would find..

In the back of the van lit up by torch beam Jenna saw three pairs of eyes blinking back at her from inside a large metal dog cage. One of them was the little black spaniel who sat wagging her tail as hard as she could! The other two dogs were a brown and white Spaniel and a black Labrador and both looked nervously from inside the cage.

After Jenna had told the officers the story of the black spaniel they seemed quite satisfied that the dog should remain with her family until its owner was located and as a large police van arrived on the road outside the car park it was followed by another car. It was Jenna's parents! Running to them Jenna burst in to tears and through sobbing words told them about Betsy running off.

"Jenna wait, it's OK, look" her mum beamed

and she turned Jenna towards the car where a tail wagging Betsy was sitting on the front seat!

"Where did you find her" Jenna wailed in relief.

"She was running down the road towards us as we drove here to find you," Karen explained hugging Jenna tightly. "What on earth is happening here?" she asked as the five men were marched past them towards the police van.

"They had Betsy and the black spaniel in the back of the van plus two other dogs" Victoria explained calmly. "We've had quite an evening!"

CHAPTER 13

As Jenna's parents spoke to the police about the other missing dogs, it was decided that the two unidentified dogs would go in the officer's car to the vets to be scanned for microchips in the hope of quickly reuniting them with their rightful owners.

The little black spaniel was very pleased to see Jenna and licked her face all over.

"Come on you, let's get you back home, you've had quite an adventure tonight." She told the dog as she stroked its soft ears.

Before she got into the car Jenna approached one of the officers and held out a still trembling hand.

"I found these," she smiled shyly as the set of keys glinted in the moonlight.

"Oh I see," said the Officer a bit confused.

"I think they might belong to that van." Jenna shrugged as she nodded her head in the direction of white van before turning on her heels and heading back to her parents' car.

When they got home Jenna fed the two dogs and sat on the floor with them for a while scratching their ears and making sure their beds were all clean and tidy. The black spaniel had started pacing the kitchen and Jenna guessed she was just a bit unsettled after an eventful evening so left them quietly in the warmth of the kitchen and headed up to her bedroom.

Grabbing her laptop and switching it on she hoped there would be some emails about the dog's possible owner. As the screen illuminated her face Jenna tightly crossed her fingers, What if there weren't any messages? There had to be!?

"You have 4 new Emails"

Clicking quickly on each one Jenna was disappointed to find that there were none about the dog.

"No way" she sighed, pushing the laptop away. She had been so sure that there would be an email from some excited owner and that the day would end on a happy note.

As she slumped back on her pillows there was a tapping at her door.

"Jenna?" It was her mum.

"Come in" Jenna called wondering if it was time for dinner.

"There's a message on the answer phone for you about the dog" her mum beamed. "It's from a lady who lost her dog a couple of years ago? She wants us to ring her back "

Jenna had totally forgotten that she had posted her home phone number on the Dog Lost website.

Racing down stairs, she re-listened to the answer phone message three times just to make sure she had written the number down correctly. With trembling fingers she dialed the number and after a slight pause the number rang.

The number rang and rang, "Please pick up!" Jenna begged.

"Hello?" a voice said. Finally an answer!

"Hi, this is Jenna Waters, you rang me about your missing dog?" Jenna asked through a shaky voice.

"Oh goodness, Yes. Wow, thank you for ringing me back so quickly" the lady continued "my name's Lydia Phillips and my dog, 'Molly,' was stolen over two years ago from our garden" She explained.

"We've just got back from holiday to find about twenty messages from my friend Vanessa about a post she had seen on the Dog Lost site. Could you tell me about this dog please? I've seen the photos you put on and there is a huge likeness between Molly and the dog you have," she continued.

Jenna explained in detail how she had found the dog on the farm and how they had taken her to the vets to be scanned for a microchip.

"The vet scanned her and found a microchip but when they called the number on the Database it was out of use."

"I've just moved house" Lydia gasped, "I didn't update the details! Please let this be Molly, I've got her microchip number here on her vaccination record. Can we compare them please that way we will know for sure?" She begged "I've never stopped hoping she would come home".

Jenna quickly grabbed the piece of paper that the vet had given her with the microchip number on it.

"OK I've got it here" Jenna said. "If you read out Molly's number I will see if they match?" she asked gently whilst keeping everything crossed that the dog who was now lying at her feet was indeed Molly.

As Lydia carefully read the long number out Jenna's hands started to shake again. They matched!

"That's right, that's her, that's Molly!" Jenna squealed and as soon as the little dog heard her real name mentioned she jumped up Jenna's legs wagging her tail like crazy!

"Hello? Lydia?" Jenna struggled to hear what Lydia was saying. It turned out she had started yelling to her husband that Molly had been found and promptly burst into tears.

"I can't believe this! I can't believe this…" Lydia sobbed.

"I've got something else to tell you too" Jenna said quietly.

"Oh OK, what's that" Lydia asked through her tears.

"Um, well, Molly is having puppies" Jenna told her.

"No way!?" Lydia sobbed "My poor dog, I don't know whether to be happy or sad". Jenna just giggled

"Well I think this is a happy thing. Not only are you getting your dog back but a few extras as well?"

Jenna's parents, hearing all the noise Jenna was

making, came to find out what was going on and as Jenna explained they cheered as well.

"That's such wonderful news love, well done" Karen said, giving her daughter a squeeze.

Through all the excitement Jenna managed to give Lydia their full address and arranged that she would come and collect Molly tomorrow evening as they lived 150 miles apart.

Finishing the phone call and promising to give Molly lots of extra fuss on her last night with the family

Jenna slid to the floor and allowed the dog to lick her face all over.

"Hello Molly!" she laughed. "'Molly the Mystery' that's what I will call you from now on."

As she fussed over both Molly and Betsy the phone rang, her dad answered and due to the excitement in the kitchen took the phone through to the hall to talk to whoever was on the other end.

When he returned he looked a bit shocked which puzzled Jenna.

"What's up?" she asked sweeping her hair back into a pony tail.

"You are not going to believe this" he said shaking his head

"What?" Jenna asked puzzled.

"Well those men the police arrested tonight over the break in here and who had the dogs?"

"Yeah, what about them?" She questioned nervously hoping it wasn't bad news.

"Well it turns out they tried to claim that Molly here was theirs!" He replied.

"What??" Jenna said angrily,

"Oh don't worry" he said "The police said the men had told them that Molly had escaped from their van a few days ago when they stopped to change a tyre, and that they had spotted us with her at the vet's and had followed us back home to get her back!"

"And what did the police say to that?" Jenna scoffed, not believing what she was hearing.

"Well the Police are now investigating where they got Molly from in the first place and it looks like they could be charged with stealing the same dog twice, as well as stealing Betsy and breaking into our house!" He laughed shaking his head. "Not the brightest of criminals!"

"No way? Jenna was dumbstruck, "I knew we were followed that night, I'm so glad they are locked up now." She shuddered. "If Zoe and I hadn't spotted their van at the Red Fox tonight we would never have seen the dogs again". Half grinning her dad tutted loudly.

"Yes, I suppose two young girls going after some dodgy men at a pub wasn't your brightest plan but at least it ended OK. Perhaps try getting hold of me or your mum next time please?" he pleaded. Jenna just winked and headed off upstairs for a hot bath.

CHAPTER 14

L ying in bed Jenna struggled to sleep. She wasn't sure if it was due to the excitement of reuniting Molly with her owner Lydia, or just the stress from the ordeal with the dog thieves.

Feeling thirsty, she threw her heavy covers back and tiptoed down to the kitchen for a glass of water. As she turned on the kitchen light and blinked at its brightness, Jenna reached for a clean glass but a strange noise made her stop. Pausing for a second she heard the noise again. It sounded like a sort of squeaking. As her eyes fully adjusted to the light she peered round the kitchen listening carefully for the sound again. As she approached Molly's bed she heard the noise again, this time louder. Molly had her back to Jenna and looked like she was washing her paws with great interest.

"What's up girl?" Jenna whispered as she knelt beside the dog's bed. "Have you injured your paw?" As she went to look closer Jenna couldn't quite believe what she was seeing.

Lying alongside Molly squirmed five shiny little bundles.

"Puppies!" Jenna gasped "Molly you clever girl!" Making a quick fuss of the dog Jenna then flew up the stairs to wake her parents.

"Jenna! What on earth....?" Her mum spluttered as Jenna flicked on their bedroom light, "Turn the light off. What's going on?" She asked crossly thinking Jenna had lost the plot completely

"We've got puppies!" Jenna sang, "five puppies, Molly's got five puppies!"

"Puppies??" Karen sat bolt upright in bed.

"Yes, puppies. Come on!" yelled Jenna as she tore back out of the bedroom and back down the stairs.

Crouching besides Molly again, Jenna tried to keep herself calm and quiet so as not to frighten the little dog. The excitement of the evening must have sent her into labour! As her parents joined her in the kitchen Jenna checked to see if the puppies were all feeding OK, which luckily they were.

"You've done a good job, you clever dog" She cooed as she gently stroked the dogs soft head.

After watching the new mum and her babies for a while they all felt that Molly was best left quiet and reluctantly headed back to bed. Morning would not come soon enough for Jenna!

Up extra early Jenna made sure that Molly had plenty of water and food next to her and took Betsy with her to go and see to Snow Prince so that Molly could eat her breakfast in peace.

The grey gelding was in particularly high spirits and exploded around the field bucking and leaping like a foal.

"Looks like someone else is excited as well!" Jenna laughed and headed back to check on the new arrivals.

Molly was such a proud mum and washed the puppies lovingly as they suckled noisily from her. There were three black puppies and two black and white spotty ones. Jenna was smitten! She decided she had best let Lydia know the good news and after another excitable phone call to her she couldn't wait for her to arrive at High Forest Farm.

Lydia was hoping to arrive around 6pm and was busily setting everything up at home for the new arrivals. Jenna was so happy that Molly was heading back to her rightful owner but also a bit sad that she wouldn't see the puppies grow up.

As darkness fell that evening Jenna, who had now been joined by an over excited Zoe, sat by the sitting room window awaiting Lydia's arrival. Every time they saw car lights the girls got to their feet but soon sat back down on the windowsill when the car drove past. Eventually they saw a car turn into the drive and Jenna knew it was Lydia. As the black 4x4 pulled up outside the front door Jenna jogged out the meet them. Lydia had bought her husband Ray with her and they both hugged Jenna before following her into the kitchen.

As soon as Lydia walked in and saw Molly lying with her puppies she burst into tears again. Gathering herself together, she approached the dog's bed.

"Molly" she called softly. The little dog's ears sprung up in recognition. "Molly, good girl, it's me" Lydia sniffed.

The little dog began to wag its tail and carefully left its bed to sniff Lydia' outstretched hand.

"Good girl, it's me" Lydia continued and after a moment of uncertainty Molly sprang up to lick her face and proceeded to leap all over her.

"Oh Wow" Jenna was now also a crying mess,

she thought her heart would melt at how Molly had recognised her owner. Zoe who was also a blubbering wreck had gone to find tissues with Karen while Jenna's dad filled Ray in on the previous night's adventures with the dog thieves. Ray and Lydia both couldn't believe what had happened and were so pleased that the men had been caught red-handed and were in police custody.

Over a cup of tea Lydia told Jenna and her family how Molly had been in the back garden of their house when two men opened the back gate and grabbed her. Lydia had heard to commotion and run out but she was too late, the men had already driven off with Molly and it was the last they had seen of her.

"We rang the police, we put her photo everywhere but there were no leads, no sightings, nothing! It was like she had vanished into thin air" She shook her head sadly. "We never gave up hope of finding her, I just can't believe I didn't update the microchip details when we moved three weeks ago. I feel so daft" she said crossly.

"We would have found you" Jenna winked. "I'm a good detective!"

"So I hear" laughed Ray, "your dad told me

about you finding the van keys and thinking to hold on to them until the police arrived"

Jenna just shrugged and blushed slightly

"I had to do something" she smirked. "Zoe helped" she grinned at best friend

"It was a joint effort".

As it got later it was decided that Lydia, Ray and Molly had best make a start on the long journey home and after an emotional goodbye Jenna helped load the puppies and Molly into the huge soft bed that Lydia had made ready for them in the back of the car.

"Please message me when you get home." Jenna asked as she fought to hold back a flood of tears.

"Of course I will." Lydia sniffed as she held Jenna tight. "We cannot thank you enough. Without you we would never have got Molly back and who knows what would have happened to her and her puppies, we will never forget what you did".

With Molly and her puppies snuggled in the back, Lydia and Ray bid the family a final farewell and drove slowly out of the drive. As the cars lights faded into the distance Jenna felt a wave of sadness and relief wash over her and as she walked back into the house with Zoe she hoped that other dogs, be it lost or stolen, would find their way home too.

THE END

TO BE CONTINUED

Look out for my next book in the High Forest farm series coming soon!

" Fly"

38413479R00061

Printed in Poland
by Amazon Fulfillment
Poland Sp. z o.o., Wrocław